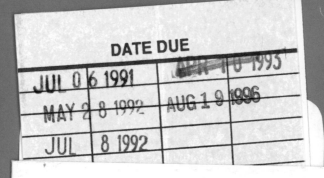

GULEESH
and the
King of France's Daughter

A Magic Lantern Fairy Tale

Retold by Neil Philip

Illustrated by Henry Underhill

Philomel Books
New York

For Roisín

It was a time of suspense, waiting and incredible excitement, those wonderful nights when the family gathered on the floor and in armchairs around the Magic Lantern to watch fairies and giants and generals perform for them in a circle of light on their very wall. Grandfather of the film projector, the Magic Lantern was first shown in Rome in 1646, but it came into its own in what is called the Golden Age of Toys when it became the darling of Victorian families. Brilliantly painted colored slides charmed Grandma and Uncle Harry as well as three-year-old Tess and ten-year-old John. Christmas, birthdays – no occasion was too large or too small to bring out the Magic Lantern. That Henry Underhill's original slides have been discovered and used to illustrate the wonderful Irish tale, *Guleesh*, revives this delight from the past for the enchantment of a new generation of children. *And now, the lantern is lit. The beam of light is aimed at the page. Begin.*

Copyright © Text: Neil Philip 1986. Copyright © Illustrations: The Albion Press Ltd 1986. Copyright © Volume: The Albion Press Ltd 1986. First American edition published in 1986 by Philomel Books, a member of The Putnam Publishing Group, 51 Madison Avenue, New York, NY 10010. Printed and bound in Italy. All Rights reserved. Designer: Emma Bradford. L.C. Number 86–9307.   ISBN 0–399–21391–0

The Albion Press would like to thank the Folklore Society for its kind permission to reproduce these lantern slides.

THERE WAS a boy in Ireland – Guleesh was his name. He had a home and parents and everything a simple lad could want. Yet his heart ached within him for something more, for something different.

On All Hallow's Eve, Guleesh went out onto the fairy hill to look at the sky and the round moon sailing so white and peaceful above him. "Oh," he sighed, "I'd sooner be any place in the world but here."

And at that moment he heard a noise like the rushing of a river in full force, or the tearing of great branches in a terrible storm. It was a host of the fairy folk, rending the air with the hubbub and turmoil of their shouts and shrieks.

Guleesh heard each fairy shouting out as loud as he could, "My horse, bridle and saddle! My horse, bridle and saddle!" and as they did so, a horse appeared for each of them.

Here's my chance, thought Guleesh. I'll have a go at that. So he shouted along with them: "My horse, bridle and saddle!" and straightaway there was a fine horse with a bridle of gold and a saddle of silver, standing before him. He leapt up on it, and as soon as he was on its back, he could see horses all round him, and the fairies on them.

"Are you coming with us tonight, Guleesh?" called one.

"I am."

"Then come along," said the little man, and off they went all together, riding like the wind, faster than the fastest horse you ever saw a-hunting, and faster than the fox with the hounds at his tail.

They overtook the cold winter's wind that was before them, and the cold winter's wind that was behind them could not catch them. They neither stopped nor stayed until they came to the brink of the sea.

Then each one of them said, "High over cap! High over cap!" and rose into the air, and Guleesh said it too and was lifted up with them.

Across the sea they flew, until they reached dry land on the other side.

They came to a palace all bright with lights. "Do you know where you are, Guleesh?" asked the little man.

"I've not a notion," said Guleesh.

"You're in France," said the little man, "and tonight the daughter of the king of France, the handsomest woman the sun ever saw, is to be married against her will. Why don't we steal her away? You're flesh and blood: if we put her up on the horse behind you, she can take a good grip, and we can save her."

"With all my heart," said Guleesh.

So they all got off their horses, and the little man said a word Guleesh did not understand, and in a blink they were in the palace, invisible to anyone.

The palace was so bright with lamps and candles, it made Guleesh's eyes hurt to look at them. The tables were so heavy with food and drink, it made Guleesh's mouth water to see them. The dancers were dancing and turning and going round so quickly and so lightly that it put a whirl in Guleesh's head to be among them. And there was so much talking and laughing and playing tricks that it seemed the happiest and best party there'd ever been.

"Which of them is the king's daughter?" asked Guleesh, and the little man pointed to her.

The rose and the lily were in her cheeks, her lips were the red of a ripe strawberry, and her hair flowed down in a river of gold. Guleesh was nearly blinded with all the loveliness and beauty he saw in her, and with the glitter of her salt tears in the candlelight.

"Oh," said Guleesh, "she is so sad, and everybody round her is so full of joy."

"She grieves," said the little man, "for tonight she must marry a man she does not love. Though indeed," he said, with a crooked little grin, "it's not a *man* she'll marry, if I can help it."

Guleesh sorely pitied the young lady then, and it broke his heart that she must marry a man she did not care for, or else be the bride of a wicked fairy.

But there was nothing he could do.

At last the dancing was over, and it was time for the wedding. The king's daughter was led to the altar that was set up in the hall, and the bridegroom was brought up too. Guleesh felt he could not bear it, when he saw him take her by the soft white hand.

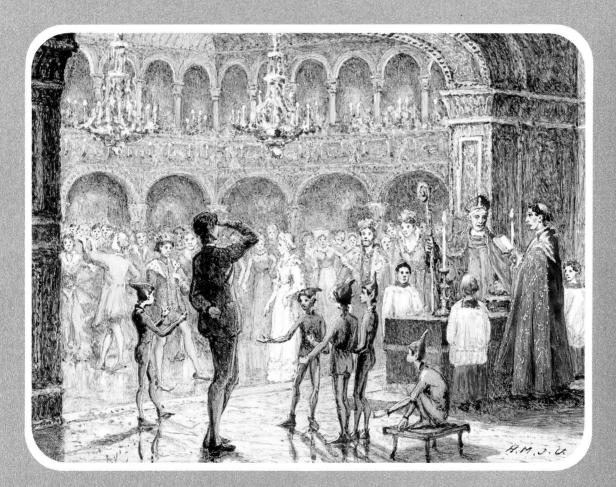

Just then, the little man said again the magic word, and the king's daughter vanished. The little man took the invisible girl by one invisible hand and Guleesh by the other, and hurried them out under the noses of the king and the queen and all the wedding party. Then the fairies and Guleesh shouted, "My horse, bridle and saddle!" and straightaway the horses were ready to ride like the wind to the brink of the sea. The king's daughter was holding on behind Guleesh, and when he shouted, "High over cap!" the horse carried them both into the air and back over the sea to Ireland.

Just as they neared the fairy hill, they passed Guleesh's house, and he saw his chance. He took the girl in his arms, and leapt from the horse.

"I call and cross you to myself in the name of God!" he said, making the sign of the cross upon her. And at that, the magic horses fell from the sky and were nothing more than the beams of old ploughs, for that was what the fairies used to make their horses.

How the fairies shrieked! They shouted, "Curse you, Guleesh, you clown, you thief. May ill-luck attend you!" Because they had no power to carry off the girl, after Guleesh had made the sign of the cross upon her.

"Oh, Guleesh, a pretty turn you did us, and we so kind to you! You'll pay us another time for this. Believe us, you'll regret it."

And the little man said, "Don't think you'll get any pleasure or profit out of the girl." As he spoke, he moved over to her and gave her a slap on the head. "I've knocked the talk out of her," he said. "Now, Guleesh, what good will she be to you dumb? You're welcome to her now." And with that he and all the fairy host disappeared.

Guleesh turned to the king's daughter and said, "They've gone. You're safe now." She made no reply.

"Lady," said Guleesh, "tell me what you want me to do. I'm not one of those fairy gentry who carried you away: I am the son of an honest farmer. If I can send you back to your father, I will."

The beautiful girl remained silent, but there were tears in her eyes and her face was flushed.

Guleesh knew that he could not take the lovely unhappy girl to his parents and say she was the King of France's daughter. They would only laugh and call him a dreamer. So he said, "I'll take you tonight to our village priest. He'll understand, and you'll be safe from any harm."

He looked into her face, and he saw the mouth moving as if she were trying to speak, but no words coming from it.

Guleesh asked, "Surely that devil hasn't really made you dumb, when he struck his nasty hand on your jaw?"

The girl raised her white smooth hand and laid her finger on her tongue to show him that she had indeed lost her voice and power of speech.

Then Guleesh took her to the priest's house and told him the whole story. When he told how she was being forced into marriage, the girl blushed, and Guleesh knew in his heart that she would rather be dumb as she was than married to a man she did not love.

So it was arranged that the girl would stay with the priest, for the moment. The priest sent letters to the King of France by every passing traveler, but all the letters went astray. And meanwhile, Guleesh and the King of France's daughter sat together every day and got on very well together without speech, for she would move her hand and fingers, wink her eyes, smile and laugh, and a thousand other things, so that he could understand her as plain as day.

So they passed a whole year, falling deeper and deeper in love every day, till it came to the last day of October. Guleesh lay on the fairy hill and thought how one year before, on Halloween, he had gone with the fairies to France and stolen away the princess.

He stayed there as night was darkening. The moon rose slowly, and it was like a knob of fire behind him; and there was a white fog rising over the fields of grass. The night was as calm as a lake when there is not a breath to move a wave on it, and there was no sound to be heard but the hoarse sudden scream of the wild geese as they passed from lake to lake, half a mile above his head, or the sharp whistle of the golden plover, rising and lying, lying and rising, as they do on a calm night. There were a thousand thousand bright stars shining over his head, and there was a little frost out, which left the grass under his foot white and crisp.

He stood there for an hour, for two hours, for three hours, while the frost took hold. And just as he turned to leave, he heard a sound far away, coming towards him. At first it was like the beating of waves on a stony shore. Then it was like the falling of a great waterfall. At last it was like a loud storm in the tops of the trees, and then the whirlwind of the fairy host burst upon him.

They were all shouting and screaming among themselves, and then in the commotion they began to cry, "My horse, bridle and saddle! My horse, bridle and saddle!" So Guleesh took courage and called out with them, "My horse, bridle and saddle!" But one of the fairies heard.

"What! Guleesh, are you here with us again? How are you getting on with your woman?" And the fairy gave out a dry little laugh. "There's no use in your calling for a horse tonight. I'll bet you won't play such a trick on us again."

"He won't," chorused the others. "He won't do it again."

Guleesh turned away, but he could still hear the fairies cackling and mocking behind him.

One said, "Isn't he the likely lad! To take a woman with him that never said as much to him as 'How do you do' since this time last year?"

"Perhaps he likes to be looking at her," said another.

"And if the dolt only knew that there's a herb growing up by his own door, which if he boiled it and gave it to her would make her well."

"That's true. That's true."

"He is a dolt."

"Don't bother your head about him. We'll be going."

And with that they rose into the air, and off they rampaged, leaving Guleesh standing there.

Guleesh didn't know what to think. Did the fairies think he was out of earshot? Or were they just careless? Or was this more of their malice? There was only one way to tell.

Guleesh did not sleep a wink, and at dawn he went out to search all round the house. It wasn't long before he did find a large strange herb growing up among the thistles and docks by the step of the house. There were seven little branches coming out of the stalk and seven leaves growing on each of them, and there was a white sap in the leaves.

Guleesh drew out his knife, cut the plant, and carried it into the house. Then he stripped the leaves off it, cut up the stalk, and squeezed out a thick white oily juice.

He put this in a pot and boiled it. And then, in case it was poison, he drank half of it. He fell to the floor and knew no more till it was night.

When Guleesh woke, he seemed to have suffered no harm, so on the next day, he took the other half of the drink to the priest's house. He gave it to the girl, and as soon as she swallowed it she fell deep asleep and would not be woken.

Guleesh and the priest sat up the entire night with the sleeping girl, between hope and despair, between expectation of saving her and fear of hurting her.

H.M.J.U.

She awoke at last when the sun had gone half its way through the heavens. She rubbed her eyes as if she did not know where she was. She did not speak.

The two men waited, but she did not speak.

At last the priest asked her, "Did you sleep well?"

And she answered him, "Very well, thank you."

No sooner did Guleesh hear her talking than he gave a shout of joy, ran over to her and fell on his two knees and said, "A thousand thanks to God, who has given you back your voice! Oh, speak again!"

And she spoke.

Now they could both tell each other of their true love, and the King of France's daughter could thank Guleesh for saving her from a forced marriage, and from the fairies, and from a life of silence. She told him she would rather stay with him, than go back to France and be a king's daughter and marry a king's son.

So all turned out well, and the fairies' wicked tricks brought happiness not sorrow to Guleesh and the King of France's daughter. The priest married them, and if they have not died they are living still.